PUFFIN BOOKS

ROALD **DAHL**'S

Mischief
and
Mayhem

Find out more about Roald Dahl
by visiting the website at
roalddahl.com

Compiled by
Kay Woodward

PUFFIN

PUFFIN BOOKS

UK | USA | Canada | Ireland | Australia
India | New Zealand | South Africa

Puffin Books is part of the Penguin Random House group of companies
whose addresses can be found at global.penguinrandomhouse.com.

puffinbooks.com

Extracts taken from: *James and the Giant Peach* first published 1961; *Matilda* first published 1988;
Charlie and the Chocolate Factory first published 1964; *The BFG* first published 1982;
The Enormous Crocodile first published 1978; *George's Marvellous Medicine* first published 1981;
Danny the Champion of the World first published 1975; *The Witches* first published 1983

First published 2013
This abridged edition published 2015
001

Text copyright © Roald Dahl Nominee Ltd, 2013
Illustrations copyright © Quentin Blake, 2013
Text design by Mandy Norman
All rights reserved

The moral right of Roald Dahl and Quentin Blake has been asserted
A CIP catalogue record for this book is available from the British Library

ISBN: 978-0-141-36663-0

The National Literacy Trust is a registered charity no. 1116260 and a company limited
by guarantee no. 5836486 registered in England and Wales and a registered charity in
Scotland no. SC042944. Registered address: 68 South Lambeth Road, London SW8 1RL.
National Literacy Trust logo and reading tips copyright © National Literacy Trust, 2015

www.literacytrust.org.uk/donate

Introduction

STOP!

Yes, you. Stop right there. Don't move.
Are you an adult? Oh, dear. I'm sorry. This book
is absolutely **NOT** meant for you. Kindly close
the pages and go and do something grown-up
instead. (Perhaps you could make a roast dinner
with a hundred vegetables or creosote a fence or
something.) Off you go. Have they gone? Good.
Hello, non-adult! This book is meant for **YOU**.
But be warned. It contains **mischief** and
mayhem of such extreme naughtiness that you
will need the cunning of Fantastic Mr Fox and the
cleverness of Matilda to continue. *You're* cunning
AND clever? Excellent. We'll get along just fine.
Now, read on.

If you've bought, borrowed or been given this **TRULY NAUGHTY** book, then you surely already know of Roald Dahl. But, just in case you're one of the 27 people on the planet who haven't heard of him, let me tell you a little more.

ROALD DAHL *was* **ONE** *of* THE BEST STORYTELLERS EVER.

There. Done. I beg your pardon? You'd like to know even more than that? Well, why didn't you say so?

Roald Dahl was born in Wales in 1916 to Norwegian parents. He had four sisters. Sadly, both his father and his eldest sister died when he was very young. And then when he wasn't much older – just nine years old – his mother sent him away to boarding school in England. Roald Dahl hated it so much that he pretended to have appendicitis so that he would be sent home. He *was* sent home.

Hurray!

But when he was found out he was sent back to school again.

Boo.

In between detention and homework and being achingly homesick, Roald spent the rest of his school years trying to outwit his **VERY STRICT** teachers and the **FORMIDABLE** matron. And testing new chocolate bars for a **VERY FAMOUS** chocolate company. Luckily, he also loved making up stories. (He wrote it all down in a book called *Boy*, if you'd like to find out EVEN MORE.)

The rest of Roald Dahl's life is like something out of a storybook too. He worked in London, which was chilly, and Africa, which wasn't. He flew fighter-planes in the Second World War, which was very scary. (Unfortunately, he crashed one in the desert, which was even scarier.) He was a spy. Shhhh. And THEN he became a writer. **Phew.**

Roald Dahl wrote stories that were funny and amazing and scary and sad. There were **unlikely heroes** and **fearsome villains**. There were funny bits and not-so-funny bits and buckets and buckets of **MISCHIEF. And MAYHEM.** Don't forget the mayhem. Was it his time at boarding school that turned him into a trickster? Was it his fabulously dark sense of humour? Was it just because he liked making people laugh? Who knows? **Roald Dahl, that's who.**

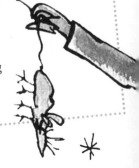

Perhaps you've already read some of Roald Dahl's books? (If not, why not? Go to your nearest library straight away, please.) If so, you'll know that they are chock-full of **HILARIOUS tricks**. Have you ever read one of his particularly mischievous tricks and – after checking that no one is watching you, of course – thought, *I could do that*? You have? Marvellous. The thing is MOST GROWN-UPS have read Roald Dahl's books too. (And if they haven't, then they're obviously numpties and not worth tricking.) So the last thing you want to do is copy one of his tricks exactly, because everyone will be expecting you to, say, superglue a hat to their head or turn their hair platinum blond just like Matilda. However, if you take one of Roald Dahl's tricks and turn it into something just a **LITTLE BIT** different, then the results can be

AMAZING.

Go on, do it.
Roald Dahl would.

In which James and his friends trick a flock of seagulls into giving them a lift.

In a few minutes everything was ready.

It was very quiet now on the top of the peach. There was nobody in sight – nobody except the Earthworm.

One half of the Earthworm, looking like a great, thick, juicy, pink sausage, lay innocently in the sun for all the seagulls to see.

The other half of him was dangling down the tunnel.

James was crouching close beside the Earthworm in the tunnel entrance, just below the surface, waiting for the first seagull. He had a loop of silk string in his hands.

The Old-Green-Grasshopper and the Ladybird were further down the tunnel, holding on to the Earthworm's tail, ready to pull him quickly in out of danger as soon as James gave the word.

And far below, in the great stone of the peach, the Glow-worm was lighting up the room so that the two spinners, the Silkworm and Miss Spider, could see what they were doing. The Centipede was down there too, exhorting them both frantically to greater efforts, and every now and again James could hear his voice coming up faintly from the depths, shouting, 'Spin, Silkworm, spin, you great fat lazy brute! Faster, faster, or we'll throw you to the sharks!'

'Here comes the first seagull!' whispered James. 'Keep still now, Earthworm. Keep still. The rest of you get ready to pull.'

'Please don't let it spike me,' begged the Earthworm.

'I won't, I won't. Ssshh . . .'

Out of the corner of one eye, James watched the seagull as it came swooping down towards the Earthworm. And then suddenly it was so close that he could see its small black eyes and its curved beak, and the beak was open, ready to grab a nice piece of flesh out of the Earthworm's back.

'Pull!' shouted James.

The Old-Green-Grasshopper and the Ladybird gave the Earthworm's tail an enormous tug, and like magic the Earthworm disappeared into the tunnel. At the same time, up went James's hand and the seagull flew right into the loop of silk that he was holding out. The loop, which had been cleverly made, tightened just the right amount (but

not too much) around its neck, and the seagull was captured.

'Hooray!' shouted the Old-Green-Grasshopper, peering out of the tunnel. 'Well done, James!'

Up flew the seagull with James paying out the silk string as it went. He gave it about fifty yards and then tied the string to the stem of the peach.

'Next one!' he shouted, jumping back into the tunnel. 'Up you get again, Earthworm! Bring up some more silk, Centipede!'

'Oh, I don't like this at all,' wailed the Earthworm. 'It only just missed me! I even felt the wind on my back as it went swishing past!'

'Ssshh!' whispered James. 'Keep still! Here comes another one!'

So they did it again.

And again, and again, and again.

And the seagulls kept coming, and James caught them one after the other and tethered them to the peach stem.

'One hundred seagulls!' he shouted, wiping the sweat from his face.

'Keep going!' they cried. 'Keep going, James!'

'Two hundred seagulls!'

'Three hundred seagulls!'

'Four hundred seagulls!'

The sharks, as though sensing that they were in danger of losing their prey, were hurling themselves at the peach more furiously than ever, and the peach was sinking lower and lower still in the water.

'Five hundred seagulls!' James shouted.

'Silkworm says she's running out of silk!' yelled the Centipede from below. 'She says she can't keep it up much longer. Nor can Miss Spider!'

'Tell them they've *got* to!' James answered. 'They can't stop now!'

'We're lifting!' somebody shouted.

'No, we're not!'

'I felt it!'

'Put on another seagull, quick!'

'Quiet, everybody! Quiet! Here's one coming now!'

This was the five hundred and first seagull, and the moment that James caught it and tethered it to the stem with all the others, the whole enormous peach suddenly started rising up slowly out of the water.

'Look out! Here we go! Hold on, boys!'

But then it stopped.

And there it hung.

It hovered and swayed, but it went no higher.

The bottom of it was just touching the water. It was like a delicately balanced scale that needed only the tiniest push to tip it one way or the other.

'One more will do it!' shouted the Old-Green-Grasshopper, looking out of the tunnel. 'We're almost there!'

And now came the big moment. Quickly, the five hundred and second seagull was caught and harnessed to the peach-stem . . .

And then suddenly . . .

But slowly . . .

Majestically . . .

Like some fabulous golden balloon . . .

With all the seagulls straining at the strings above . . .

The giant peach rose up dripping out of the water and began climbing towards the heavens.

But don't do that, do THIS!

TRiCK

The Booby-trapped Peach

Unless you happen to have a giant-fruit-and-veg shop nearby, you're unlikely to have a giant peach. (Or a giant earthworm, for that matter.) **DON'T PANIC**. For this trick, you will need one average, run-of-the-mill, really quite normal-sized peach, available from all good fruit-and-veg shops. But it must be VERY RIPE.

Why did the peach stop at the top of the hill? **Because it ran out of juice.**

YOU WILL NEED:
☆ One ripe peach
☆ One jelly worm (the edible sort)
☆ One cocktail stick or a toothpick
☆ One fruit bowl

WHAT YOU DO:

1 Being VERY careful, **spear your peach** with a cocktail stick or toothpick and wiggle it about a bit so that you've made a small tunnel in your sticky, juicy fruit.

2 **Poke the jelly worm into the tunnel**. Leave a little bit of the worm sticking out of the peach, just like in *James and the Giant Peach*.

3 Put the **booby-trapped peach** into the fruit bowl.

4 Wait.

5 If a grown-up does not immediately decide that they would like to sink their teeth into a delicious peach then you may have to **fill their heads with fruity, sticky, juicy thoughts** until they can stand it no longer and simply have to eat a peach RIGHT NOW.

6 Get ready to double up with laughter when the grown-up bites into the ripe peach and thinks they have eaten **A REAL LIVE EARTHWORM**.

7 **Double up with laughter. Or run.**

The Platinum-Blond Man

In which Matilda swaps OIL OF VIOLETS HAIR TONIC for PLATINUM BLONDE HAIR-DYE EXTRA STRONG and makes her father see RED. Actually, yellow. Hmm. Blond, really.

Mr Wormwood kept his hair looking bright and strong, or so he thought, by rubbing into it every morning large quantities of a lotion called OIL OF VIOLETS HAIR TONIC. A bottle of this smelly purple mixture always stood on the shelf above the sink in the bathroom alongside all the toothbrushes, and a very vigorous scalp massage with OIL OF VIOLETS took place daily after shaving was completed. This hair and scalp massage was always accompanied by loud masculine grunts and heavy breathing and gasps of 'Ahhh, that's better! That's the stuff! Rub it right into the roots!' which could be clearly heard by Matilda in her bedroom across the corridor.

Now, in the early morning privacy of the bathroom, Matilda unscrewed the cap of her father's OIL OF VIOLETS and tipped three-quarters of the contents down the drain. Then she filled the bottle up with her mother's PLATINUM BLONDE HAIR-DYE EXTRA STRONG. She carefully left enough of her father's original hair tonic in the bottle so that when she gave it a good shake the whole thing still looked reasonably purple. She then replaced the bottle on the shelf above the sink, taking care to put her mother's bottle back in the cupboard. So far so good.

At breakfast time Matilda sat quietly at the dining-room table eating her cornflakes. Her brother sat opposite her with his back to the door devouring hunks of bread smothered with a mixture of peanut-butter and strawberry jam. The mother was just out of sight around the corner in the kitchen making Mr

Wormwood's breakfast which always had to be two fried eggs on fried bread with three pork sausages and three strips of bacon and some fried tomatoes.

At this point Mr Wormwood came noisily into the room. He was incapable of entering any room quietly, especially at breakfast time. He always had to make his appearance felt immediately by creating a lot of noise and clatter. One could almost hear him saying, 'It's me! Here I come, the great man himself, the master of the house, the wage-earner, the one who makes it possible for all the rest of you to live so well! Notice me and pay your respects!'

On this occasion he strode in and slapped his son on the back and shouted, 'Well, my boy, your father feels he's in for another great money-making day today at the garage! I've got a few little beauties I'm going to flog to the idiots this morning. Where's my breakfast?'

'It's coming, treasure,' Mrs Wormwood called from the kitchen.

Matilda kept her face bent low over her cornflakes. She didn't dare look up. In the first place she wasn't at all sure what she was going to see. And secondly, if she did see what she thought she was going to see, she wouldn't trust herself to keep a straight face. The son was looking directly ahead out of the window stuffing himself with bread and peanut-butter and strawberry jam.

The father was just moving round to sit at the head of the table when the mother came sweeping out from the kitchen carrying a huge plate piled high with eggs and sausages and bacon and tomatoes. She looked up. She caught sight of her husband. She stopped dead. Then she let out a scream that seemed to lift her right up into the air and she dropped the plate with a crash and a splash on to the floor. Everyone jumped, including Mr Wormwood.

'What the heck's the matter with you, woman?' he shouted. 'Look at the mess you've made on the carpet!'

'Your hair!' the mother was shrieking, pointing a quivering finger at her husband. 'Look at your *hair*! What've you done to your *hair*?'

'What's wrong with my hair, for heaven's sake?' he said.

'Oh my gawd, Dad, what've you done to your hair?' the son shouted.

A splendid noisy scene was building up nicely in the breakfast room.

Matilda said nothing. She simply sat there admiring the wonderful effect of her own handiwork. Mr Wormwood's fine crop of black hair was now a dirty silver, the colour this time of a tightrope-walker's tights that had not been washed for the entire circus season.

'You've . . . you've . . . you've *dyed* it!' shrieked the mother. 'Why did you do it, you fool! It looks absolutely frightful! It looks horrendous! You look like a freak!'

'What the blazes are you all talking about?' the father yelled, putting both hands to his hair. 'I most certainly have not dyed it! What d'you mean I've dyed it? What's happened to it? Or is this some sort of a stupid joke?' His face was turning pale green, the colour of sour apples.

'You must have dyed it, Dad,' the son said. 'It's the same colour as Mum's, only much dirtier-looking.'

'Of course he's dyed it!' the mother cried. 'It can't change colour all by itself! What on earth were you trying to do, make yourself look handsome or something? You look like someone's grandmother gone wrong!'

'Get me a mirror!' the father yelled. 'Don't just stand there shrieking at me! Get me a mirror!'

The mother's handbag lay on a chair at the other end of the table. She opened the bag and got out a powder compact that had a small round mirror on the inside of the lid. She opened the compact and handed it to her husband. He grabbed it and held it before his face and in doing so spilled most of the powder all over the front of his fancy tweed jacket.

'Be *careful*!' shrieked the mother. 'Now look what you've done! That's my best Elizabeth Arden face powder!'

'Oh my gawd!' yelled the father, staring into the little mirror. 'What's happened to me! I look terrible! I look just like *you* gone wrong! I can't go down to the garage and sell cars like this! How did it happen?' He stared round the room, first at the mother, then at the son, then at Matilda. 'How *could* it have happened?' he yelled.

'I imagine, Daddy,' Matilda said quietly, 'that you weren't looking very hard and you simply took Mummy's bottle of hair stuff off the shelf instead of your own.'

'Of *course* that's what happened!' the mother cried. 'Well really, Harry, how stupid can you get? Why didn't you read the label before you started splashing the stuff all over you! Mine's *terribly* strong. I'm only meant to use one tablespoon of it in a whole basin of water and you've gone and put it all over your head neat! It'll probably take all your hair off in the end! Is your scalp beginning to burn, dear?'

'You mean I'm going to lose all my hair?' the husband yelled.

'I think you will,' the mother said. 'Peroxide is a very powerful chemical. It's what they put down the lavatory to disinfect the pan, only they give it another name.'

'What are you saying!' the husband cried. 'I'm not a lavatory pan! I don't want to be disinfected!'

'Even diluted like I use it,' the mother told him, 'it makes a good deal of my hair fall out, so goodness knows what's going to happen to you. I'm surprised it didn't take the whole of the top of your head off!'

'What shall I do?' wailed the father. 'Tell me quick what to do before it starts falling out!'

Matilda said, 'I'd give it a good wash, Dad, if I were you, with soap and water. But you'll have to hurry.'

'Will that change the colour back?' the father asked anxiously.

'Of course it won't, you twit,' the mother said.

'Then what do I do? I can't go around looking like this for ever!'

'You'll have to have it dyed black,' the mother said. 'But wash it first or there won't be any there to dye.'

'Right!' the father shouted, springing into action. 'Get me an appointment with your hairdresser this instant for a hair-dyeing job! Tell them it's an emergency! They've got to boot someone else off their list! I'm going upstairs to wash it now!' With that the man dashed out of the room and Mrs Wormwood, sighing deeply, went to the telephone to call the beauty parlour.

'He does do some pretty silly things now and again, doesn't he, Mummy?' Matilda said.

The mother, dialling the number on the phone, said, 'I'm afraid men are not always quite as clever as they think they are. You will learn that when you get a bit older, my girl.'

But don't do that, do THIS!

TRiCK

Surprise Shampoo

When Roald Dahl
wrote *Matilda*, he claimed that

Oil of Violets Hair Tonic and

**PLATINUM BLONDE HAIR-DYE
EXTRA STRONG**

could be found in every hairdresser and every
barbershop around the world. Now, they're all gone.
Every single bottle. Don't ask me why. As a writer he
sometimes made things up. And don't panic either.
For different hair effects, try adding these wonderful
ingredients to the nearest shampoo bottle.
Spectacular results are guaranteed.

★ ★ ★

What's the only
kind of poo that
doesn't smell
horrible?
Shampoo!

 Add two teaspoons of **GLITTER** for super-sparkly hair.

 Add a few drops of **FOOD COLOURING** for red or yellow or green or blue or purple hair.

 Or just fill an empty bottle with **CUSTARD**. When applied to hair, this yellow gloop will not make the hair glossy or shiny or sparkly or highlighted. It will not condition dry hair and it will not mean that the owner of long princess hair can swing it round their shoulders in a big curtain of loveliness as if they are starring in a television advert. **It will just look as if a giant bird has pooped on their head.** And how funny would that be?

Augustus Gloop

Goes up the Pipe

In which Augustus Gloop learns that drinking from a chocolate river is delicious yet VERY DANGEROUS.

When Mr Wonka turned round and saw what Augustus Gloop was doing, he cried out, 'Oh, no! *Please*, Augustus, *please*! I beg of you not to do that. My chocolate must be untouched by human hands!'

'Augustus!' called out Mrs Gloop. 'Didn't you hear what the man said? Come away from that river at once!'

'This stuff is fabulous!' said Augustus, taking not the slightest notice of his mother or Mr Wonka. 'Gosh, I need a bucket to drink it properly!'

'Augustus,' cried Mr Wonka, hopping up and down and waggling his stick in the air, 'you *must* come away. You are dirtying my chocolate!'

24

'Augustus!' cried Mrs Gloop.

'Augustus!' cried Mr Gloop.

But Augustus was deaf to everything except the call of his enormous stomach. He was now lying full length on the ground with his head far out over the river, lapping up the chocolate like a dog.

'Augustus!' shouted Mrs Gloop. 'You'll be giving that nasty cold of yours to about a million people all over the country!'

'Be careful, Augustus!' shouted Mr Gloop. 'You're leaning too far out!'

Mr Gloop was absolutely right. For suddenly there was a shriek, and then a splash, and into the river went Augustus Gloop, and in one second he had disappeared under the brown surface.

'Save him!' screamed Mrs Gloop, going white in the face, and waving her umbrella about. 'He'll drown! He can't swim a yard! Save him! Save him!'

'Good heavens, woman,' said Mr Gloop, 'I'm not diving in there! I've got my best suit on!'

Augustus Gloop's face came up again to the surface,

painted brown with chocolate. 'Help! Help! Help!' he yelled. 'Fish me out!'

'Don't just *stand* there!' Mrs Gloop screamed at Mr Gloop. '*Do* something!'

'I *am* doing something!' said Mr Gloop, who was now taking off his jacket and getting ready to dive into the chocolate. But while he was doing this, the wretched boy was being sucked closer and closer towards the mouth of one of the great pipes that was dangling down into the river. Then all at once, the powerful suction took hold of him completely, and he was pulled under the surface and then into the mouth of the pipe.

The crowd on the riverbank waited breathlessly to see where he would come out.

'*There he goes!*' somebody shouted, pointing upwards.

And sure enough, because the pipe was made of glass, Augustus Gloop could be clearly seen shooting up inside it, head first, like a torpedo.

'Help! Murder! Police!' screamed Mrs Gloop. 'Augustus, come back at once! Where are you going?'

'It's a wonder to me,' said Mr Gloop, 'how that pipe is big enough for him to go through it.'

'It *isn't* big enough!' said Charlie Bucket. 'Oh dear, look! He's slowing down!'

'So he is!' said Grandpa Joe.

'He's going to stick!' said Charlie.

'I think he is!' said Grandpa Joe.

'By golly, he *has* stuck!' said Charlie.

'It's his stomach that's done it!' said Mr Gloop.

'He's blocked the whole pipe!' said Grandpa Joe.

'Smash the pipe!' yelled Mrs Gloop, still waving her umbrella. 'Augustus, come out of there at once!'

The watchers below could see the chocolate swishing around the boy in the pipe, and they could see it building up behind him in a solid mass, pushing against the blockage. The pressure was terrific. Something had to give. Something did give, and that something was Augustus. *WHOOF!* Up he shot again like a bullet in the barrel of a gun.

But don't do that, do THIS!

TRICK

The Hot Chocolate That Isn't

Everyone* loves chocolate. So why not take advantage of this fact and play a **FIENDISHLY** naughty trick on someone who simply adores the stuff?

*And if they don't, they clearly need a trip to a chocolate factory to sort them out.

What's the best thing to put into a chocolate pie? **Your teeth.**

YOU WILL NEED:

⭐ Two mugs

⭐ Four teaspoons of drinking chocolate

⭐ Two teaspoons of gravy granules

WHAT YOU DO:

1 Offer to make **hot chocolate** for an adult who loves chocolate.

2 Make a mug of deliciously chocolatey hot chocolate using two teaspoons of drinking chocolate. (Ask an older person who's in on the trick to supervise the hot water or hot milk. You really don't want to spill it on yourself.)

3 Make another mug of deliciously chocolatey hot chocolate using two teaspoons of drinking chocolate **AND two teaspoons of gravy granules**. Stir well.

4 Now take the two drinks into the room where your unsuspecting adult is waiting.

5 Give the mug of choco-gravy to the adult and (this is VERY important) keep the mug of real hot chocolate for yourself.

6 Sip the hot chocolate and say, **'Mmmmmmmmmmm . . .'**

7 Wait for your victim to say, **'BLEURGHHHHHH!'**

Capture

In which Sophie is VERY BRAVE and, with the help of the BFG, tackles a VERY BIG and VERY UNFRIENDLY giant.

Sophie ran up behind the Fleshlumpeater. She was holding the brooch between her fingers. When she was right up close to the great naked hairy legs, she rammed the three-inch-long pin of the brooch as hard as she could into the Fleshlumpeater's right ankle. It went deep into the flesh and stayed there.

The giant gave a roar of pain and jumped high in the air. He dropped the soldier and made a grab for his ankle.

The BFG, knowing what a coward the Fleshlumpeater was, saw his chance. 'You is bitten by a snake!' he shouted. 'I seed it biting you! It was a frightsome poisnowse viper! It was a dreadly dungerous vindscreen viper!'

'Save our souls!' bellowed the Fleshlumpeater. 'Sound the crumpets! I is bitten by a septicous venomsome vindscreen viper!' He flopped to the ground and sat there howling his head off and clutching his ankle with both hands. His fingers felt the brooch. 'The teeth of the dreadly viper is still sticking into me!' he yelled. 'I is feeling the teeth sticking into my anklet!'

The BFG saw his second chance. 'We must be getting those viper's teeth out at once!' he cried. 'Otherwise you is deader than duck-soup! I is helping you!'

The BFG knelt down beside the Fleshlumpeater. 'You must grab your anklet very tight with both hands!' he ordered. 'That will stop the poisnowse juices from the venomsome viper going up your leg and into your heart!'

The Fleshlumpeater grabbed his ankle with both hands.

'Now close your eyes and grittle your teeth and look up to heaven and say your prayers while I is taking out the teeth of the venomsome viper,' the BFG said.

The terrified Fleshlumpeater did exactly as he was told.

The BFG signalled for some rope. A soldier rushed

it over to him. With both the Fleshlumpeater's hands gripping his ankle, it was a simple matter for the BFG to tie the ankles and hands together with a tight knot.

'I is pulling out the frightsome viper's teeth!' the BFG said as he pulled the knot tight.

'Do it quickly!' shouted the Fleshlumpeater, 'before I is pizzened to death!'

'There we is,' said the BFG, standing up. 'You can look now.'

When the Fleshlumpeater saw that he was trussed up like a turkey, he gave a yell so loud that the heavens trembled. He rolled and he wriggled, he fought and he figgled, he squirmed and he squiggled. But there was not a thing he could do.

'Well done you!' Sophie cried.

'Well done *you*!' said the BFG, smiling down at the little girl. 'You is saving all of our lives!'

'Will you please get that brooch back for me,' Sophie said. 'It belongs to the Queen.'

But don't do that, do THIS!

TRICK

Four Ways To Trick A Giant

Unless you live in a land of thick forests and rushing rivers and hills as bare as concrete and ground that is flat and pale yellow, with great lumps of blue rock scattered around and dead trees standing around like skeletons – which is the land where the **BFG** lives – then you are unlikely to meet a real live **giant**. So the next biggest thing is a really tall grown-up. Trick one of those instead!

1 **Take the batteries out of the TV remote control.** Hide them. Replace the remote control. Now it will be more entertaining watching the grown-up trying to make the TV work than the TV itself! (For an even better trick, secretly replace the batteries and then tell the grown-up that they must have been doing it wrong, because – look! – the remote control is working **PERFECTLY**.)

2 **Stuff newspaper inside shoes.** Make sure it's right down at the toes so the grown-up doesn't see it before they put their feet in. Fill **ALL** shoes and boots, even ones that the grown-up hardly ever wears, for fun **ALL THROUGH THE YEAR.** How they'll laugh!

3 **Change the time on the clocks.** All of the clocks. Get up really early one morning and move them an hour forward. Then **EVERYONE** will be an hour early for work and school. Except you. You can have a lie-in. **Bwa-ha-haaa!**

4 **Press the volume button on the TV remote control** to the loudest it will go when it is turned off. The next person who turns on the TV will have the **FRIGHT OF HIS OR HER LIFE!**

> When is a magician in a car not a magician in a car?
> **When he turns into a driveway.**

The Marvellous Plan

In which George decides to make his very own magic medicine to treat his horrid grandma.

George sat himself down at the table in the kitchen. He was shaking a little. Oh, how he hated Grandma! He really *hated* that horrid old witchy woman. And all of a sudden he had a tremendous urge to *do something* about her. Something *whopping*. Something *absolutely terrific*. A *real shocker*. A sort of explosion. He wanted to blow away the witchy smell that hung about her in the next room. He may have been only eight years old but he was a brave little boy. He was ready to take this old woman on.

'I'm not going to be frightened by *her*,' he said softly to himself. But he *was* frightened. And that's why he wanted suddenly to explode her away.

Well . . . not quite away. But he did want to shake the old woman up a bit.

Very well, then. What should it be, this whopping terrific exploding shocker for Grandma?

He would have liked to put a firework banger under her chair but he didn't have one.

He would have liked to put a long green snake down the back of her dress but he didn't have a long green snake.

He would have liked to put six big black rats in the room with her and lock the door but he didn't have six big black rats.

As George sat there pondering this interesting problem, his eye fell upon the bottle of Grandma's brown medicine standing on the sideboard. Rotten stuff it seemed to be. Four times a day a large spoonful of it was shovelled into her mouth and it didn't do her the slightest bit of good. She was always just as horrid after she'd had it as she'd been before.

The whole point of medicine, surely, was to make a person better. If it didn't do that, then it was quite useless.

So-ho! thought George suddenly. *Ah-ha! Hohum!* I know exactly what I'll do. I shall make her a *new* medicine, one that is so strong and so fierce and so fantastic it will either cure her completely or blow off the top of her head. I'll make her a *magic medicine*, a medicine no doctor in the world has ever made before.

George looked at the kitchen clock. It said five past ten. There was nearly an hour left before Grandma's next dose was due at eleven.

'Here we go, then!' cried George, jumping up from the table. 'A magic medicine it shall be!'

'So give me a bug and a jumping flea,
Give me two snails and lizards three,
And a slimy squiggler from the sea,
And the poisonous sting of a bumblebee,
And the juice from the fruit of the ju-jube
      tree,
And the powdered bone of a wombat's
      knee.
And one hundred other things as well
Each with a rather nasty smell.

I'll stir them up, I'll boil them long,
A mixture tough, a mixture strong.
And then, heigh-ho, and down it goes,
A nice big spoonful (hold your nose)
Just gulp it down and have no fear.
"How do you like it, Granny dear?"
Will she go pop? Will she explode?
Will she go flying down the road?
Will she go poof in a puff of smoke?
Start fizzing like a can of Coke?
Who knows? Not I. Let's wait and see.
(I'm glad it's neither you nor me.)
Oh Grandma, if you only knew
What I have got in store for you!'

But don't do that, do THIS!

TRICK

A Recipe for Chocolate and Brussels Sprout Pie

It's a well-known fact that grown-ups adore eating vegetables nearly as much as they adore making younger people eat vegetables. So they are bound to LOVE this delightful pie. Why not rustle one up at the weekend, feed it to the grown-ups of your choice and THEN get them to guess what's in it?

PS If they make lots of weird noises like **BLEURGH** and **EEUCH**, tell them that it's good for them and not to whinge. Just like they tell you.

YOU WILL NEED:

☆ One spoonful of butter or margarine or posh spread made from olives

☆ One pie dish

☆ One rolling pin

☆ One packet of puff pastry

☆ One bag of Brussels sprouts

☆ One bar of very dark chocolate

☆ One egg

☆ One oven

☆ One group of grown-ups, preferably the healthy sort

OPTIONAL INGREDIENTS:
Cabbage, Marmite, chocolate sprinkles, syrup, baked beans, puréed pumpkin, jam, tinned carrots and sardines. Mmm.

WHAT YOU DO:

1 **Rub** the butter, margarine or posh spread made from olives into your pie dish.

2 **Roll out two circles of pastry.** Put one of them into your pie dish.

3 Put the **Brussels sprouts** into the pie dish.

4 Break the **chocolate** up into squares and put that in too.

5 Add as many of the optional ingredients as you like.

6 Place the other circle of pastry on top of the pie dish and **seal the pastry round the edges** by pinching them together.

7 **Paint the top of the pie** with beaten egg, just to make it look super appetizing when it's cooked.

8 **Ask an adult to help you pop it in the oven.** Bake for 45 minutes to an hour at 190° C or Gas Mark 5.

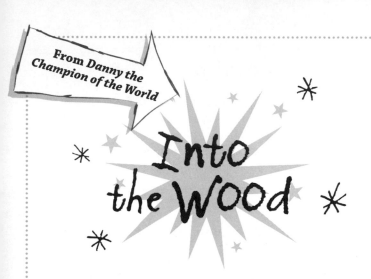

From Danny the
Champion of the World

Into the Wood

In which Danny and his father risk life, limb and bottom to poach pheasants from right under the nose of the gamekeeper.

We crouched close to the ground, watching the keeper. He was a smallish man with a cap on his head and a big double-barrelled shotgun under his arm. He never moved. He was like a little post standing there.

'Should we go?' I whispered.

The keeper's face was shadowed by the peak of his cap, but it seemed to me he was looking straight at us.

'Should we go, Dad?'

'Hush,' my father said.

Slowly, never taking his eyes from the keeper, he reached into his pocket and brought out a single raisin. He placed it in the palm of his right hand, and then quickly with a little flick of the wrist he threw the raisin high into the air. I watched it as it went sailing over the bushes and I saw it land within a yard of two hen birds standing beside an old tree-stump. Both birds turned their heads sharply at the drop of the raisin. Then one of them hopped over and made a quick peck at the ground and that must have been it.

I looked at the keeper. He hadn't moved.

I could feel a trickle of cold sweat running down one side of my forehead and across my cheek. I didn't dare lift a hand to wipe it away.

My father threw a second raisin into the clearing . . . then a third . . . and a fourth . . . and a fifth.

It takes guts to do that, I thought. Terrific guts. If I'd been alone I would never have stayed there for one second. But my father was in a sort of poacher's trance. For him, this was it. This was the moment of danger, the biggest thrill of all.

He kept on throwing the raisins into the clearing, swiftly, silently, one at a time. Flick went his wrist, and up went the raisin, high over the bushes, to land among the pheasants.

Then all at once, I saw the keeper turn away his head to inspect the wood behind him.

My father saw it too. Quick as a flash, he pulled the bag of raisins out of his pocket and tipped the whole lot into the palm of his right hand.

'Dad!' I whispered. 'Don't!'

But with a great sweep of the arm he flung the entire handful way over the bushes into the clearing.

They fell with a soft little patter, like raindrops on dry leaves, and every single pheasant in the place must have heard them fall. There was a flurry of wings and a rush to find the treasure.

The keeper's head flicked round as though there were a spring inside his neck. The birds were all pecking away madly at the raisins. The keeper took two quick paces forward, and for a moment I thought he was going in to investigate. But then he stopped, and his face came up and his eyes began travelling slowly round the edge of the clearing.

'Lie down flat!' my father whispered. 'Stay there! Don't move an inch!'

I flattened my body against the ground and pressed one side of my face into the brown leaves. The soil below the leaves had a queer pungent smell, like beer. Out of one eye, I saw my father raise his head just a tiny bit to watch the keeper. He kept watching him.

'Don't you *love* this?' he whispered to me.

I didn't dare answer him.

We lay there for what seemed like a hundred years.

At last I heard my father whisper, 'Panic's over. Follow me, Danny. But be extra careful, he's still there. And *keep down low all the time.*'

He started crawling away quickly on his hands and knees. I went after him. I kept thinking of the keeper who was somewhere behind us. I was very conscious of that keeper, and I was also very conscious of my own backside, and how it was sticking up in the air for all to see. I could understand now why 'poacher's bottom' was a fairly common complaint in this business.

We went along on our hands and knees for about a hundred yards.

'Now run!' my father said.

We got to our feet and ran, and a few minutes later we came out through the hedge into the lovely open safety of the cart-track.

'It went marvellously!' my father said, breathing heavily. 'Didn't it go absolutely marvellously?' His face was scarlet and glowing with triumph.

'Did the keeper see us?' I asked.

'Not on your life!' he said. 'And in a few minutes the sun will be going down and the birds will all be flying up to roost and that keeper will be sloping off home to his supper. Then all we've got to do is go back in again and help ourselves. We'll be picking them up off the ground like pebbles!'

He sat down on the grassy bank below the hedge. I sat down close to him. He put an arm round my shoulders and gave me a hug. 'You did well, Danny,' he said. 'I'm right proud of you.'

But don't do that, do THIS!

TRICK

Poach an Egg, Not a Pheasant

Poach an egg. (Ask an adult to help with the hot-water bit.) It's easier than poaching pheasants – and a lot more legal. Better still, boil an egg for a **REALLY good yolk**. (Ha ha! Ahem. Sorry – joke, not yolk.) Pop the hard-boiled egg back in the egg box when you're done. Then be ready to laugh **REALLY LOUDLY** when someone tries to crack it.

From

The Enormous Crocodile

*In which the Enormous Crocodile creates the
world's best fancy-dress outfit EVER.*

The Enormous Crocodile crept over to a place where
there were a lot of coconut trees.

He knew that children from the town often came
here looking for coconuts. The trees were too tall for
them to climb, but there were always some coconuts
on the ground that had fallen down.

The Enormous Crocodile quickly collected all
the coconuts that were lying on the ground. He also
gathered together several fallen branches.

'Now for Clever Trick Number One!' he whispered
to himself. 'It won't be long before I am eating the first
part of my lunch!'

He took all the coconut branches and held them
between his teeth.

He grasped the coconuts in his front paws. Then he stood straight up in the air, balancing himself on his tail.

He arranged the branches and the coconuts so cleverly that he now looked exactly like a small coconut tree standing among the big coconut trees.

Soon, two children came along. They were brother and sister. The boy was called Toto. His sister was called Mary. They walked around looking for fallen coconuts, but they couldn't find any because the Enormous Crocodile had gathered them all up.

'Oh look!' cried Toto. 'That tree over there is much smaller than the others! And it's full of coconuts! I think I could climb that one quite easily if you help me up the first bit.'

Toto and Mary ran towards what they thought was the small coconut tree.

The Enormous Crocodile peered through the branches, watching them as they came closer and closer. He licked his lips. He began to dribble with excitement.

Suddenly there was a tremendous whooshing noise. It was Humpy-Rumpy, the Hippopotamus. He came crashing and snorting out of the jungle. His head was down low and he was galloping at a terrific speed.

'Look out, Toto!' shouted Humpy-Rumpy. 'Look out, Mary! That's not a coconut tree! It's the Enormous Crocodile and he wants to eat you up!'

But don't do that, do THIS!

TRiCK

How to Disguise Yourself as a Coconut Tree

Don't be put off by the title. This really is a very simple trick, as long as you have the following everyday items to hand.

> **YOU WILL NEED:**
> ☆ One speedboat (but don't worry if you haven't got a speedboat – a helicopter will do just fine)
> ☆ One desert island
> ☆ 50 metres of coconut matting
> ☆ 34 coconut leaves
> ☆ One helper

WHAT YOU DO:

1 Travel to the desert island by **speedboat** or **helicopter**.

2 Ask your helper to **roll you up in the coconut matting**, but make sure your head is poking out of the top. Otherwise, it could get a bit boring in there.

3 Ask your helper to stick the **34 coconut leaves** at the top of the matting, so that they sprout outwards like A REAL TREE, while cunningly hiding your head at the same time.

4 **There. You're done.**

5 Um . . . watch helplessly as your helper escapes from the desert island in the speedboat or the helicopter and leaves you stranded there.

6 **Cheer up!** That's a fabulous outfit. You look JUST LIKE a coconut tree. **Bravo!**

The Recipe

In which The Grand High Witch describes the spell that will turn children into mice at PRECISELY nine o'clock the next morning, just in time for school.

'Attention again!' The Grand High Witch was shouting. 'I vill now give to you the rrrecipe for concocting Formula 86 Delayed Action Mouse-Maker! Get out pencils and paper.'

Handbags were opened all over the room and notebooks were fished out.

'Give us the recipe, O Brainy One!' cried the audience impatiently. 'Tell us the secret.'

'First,' said The Grand High Witch, 'I had to find something that vould cause the children to become very small very qvickly.'

'And what was that?' cried the audience.

'That part vos simple,' said The Grand High Witch. 'All you have to do if you are vishing to make a child very small is to look at him through the wrrrong end of a telescope.'

'She's a wonder!' cried the audience. 'Who else would have thought of a thing like that?'

'So you take the wrrrong end of a telescope,' continued The Grand High Witch, 'and you boil it until it gets soft.'

'How long does that take?' they askcd her.

'Tventy-vun hours of boiling,' answered The Grand High Witch. 'And vhile this is going on, you take exactly forty-five brrrown mice and you chop off their tails vith a carving-knife and you fry the tails in hair-oil until they are nice and crrrisp.'

'What do we do with all those mice who have had their tails chopped off?' asked the audience.

'You simmer them in frog-juice for vun hour,' came the answer. 'But listen to me. So far I have only given you the easy part of the rrrecipe. The rrreally difficult problem is to put in something that vill have a genuine delayed action rrree-sult, something that can be eaten by children on a certain day but vhich vill not start vurrrking on them until nine o'clock the next morning vhen they arrive at school.'

'What did you come up with, O Brainy One?' they called out. 'Tell us the great secret!'

'The secret,' announced The Grand High Witch triumphantly, 'is an *alarm-clock*!'

'An alarm-clock!' they cried. 'It's a stroke of genius!'

'Of course it is,' said The Grand High Witch.

'You can set a tventy-four-hour alarm-clock today and at exactly nine o'clock tomorrow it vill go off.'

'But we will need five million alarm-clocks!' cried the audience. 'We will need one for each child!'

'Idiots!' shouted The Grand High Witch. 'If you are vonting a steak, you do not cook the whole cow! It is the same vith alarm-clocks. Vun clock vill make enough for a thousand children. Here is vhat you do. You set your alarm-clock to go off at nine o'clock tomorrow morning.

Then you rrroast it in the oven until it is crrrisp and tender. Are you wrrriting this down?'

'We are, Your Grandness, we are!' they cried.

'Next,' said The Grand High Witch, 'you take your boiled telescope and your frrried mouse-tails and your cooked mice and your rrroasted alarm-clock and all together you put them into the mixer. Then you mix

them at full speed. This vill give you a nice thick paste. Vhile the mixer is still mixing you must add to it the yolk of vun grrruntle's egg.'

'A gruntle's egg!' cried the audience. 'We shall do that!'

Underneath all the clamour that was going on I heard one witch in the back row saying to her neighbour, 'I'm getting a bit old to go bird's nesting. Those ruddy gruntles always nest very high up.'

'So you mix in the egg,' The Grand High Witch went on, 'and vun after the other you also mix in the following items: the claw of a crrrabcrrruncher, the beak of a blabbersnitch, the snout of a grrrobblesqvirt and the tongue of a catsprrringer.

I trust you are not having any trrrouble finding those.'

'None at all!' they cried out. 'We will spear the blabbersnitch and trap the crabcruncher and shoot the grobblesquirt and catch the catspringer in his burrow!'

'Excellent!' said The Grand High Witch. 'Vhen you have mixed everything together in the mixer, you vill have a most marvellous-looking grrreen liqvid. Put vun drop, just vun titchy droplet, of this liqvid into a chocolate or a sveet, and *at nine o'clock the next morning* the child who ate it vill turn into a mouse in tventy-six seconds! But vun vurd of vorning. Never increase the dose. Never put more than vun drrrop into each sveet or chocolate. And never give more than vun sweet or chocolate to each child. An overdose of Delayed Action Mouse-Maker vill mess up the timing of the alarm-clock and cause the child to turn into a mouse too early. A large overdose might even have an instant effect, and you vouldn't vont that, vould you? You vouldn't vont the children turning into mice rrrright there in your sveet-shops. That vould give the game away. So be very carrreful! Do not overdose!'

But don't do that, do THIS!

TriCK

The Great Mouse Trick

THE GRAND HIGH WITCH'S
Formula 86 Delayed Action Mouse-Maker

is probably not a spell you want to cast on your friends. (Not if you ever want them to speak – or even **SQUEAK** – to you again.) Instead, try this harmless yet **HILARIOUS** trick. All you need to do is stick a tiny piece of sticky tape over the optical sensor underneath a computer mouse and, as if by magic, it won't work.